the Shoe Box

the Shoe Box

{ A Christmas Story }

FRANCINE RIVERS

TYNDALE HOUSE PUBLISHERS, INC.
CAROL STREAM, ILLINOIS

Visit Tyndale's exciting Web site at www.tyndale.com.

Check out the latest about Francine Rivers at www.francinerivers.com.

TYNDALE and Tyndale's quill logo are registered trademarks of Tyndale House Publishers, Inc.

The Shoe Box

Designed by Beth Sparkman

Published in association with the literary agency of Browne & Miller Literary Associates, LLC, 410 Michigan Avenue, Suite 460, Chicago, IL 60605.

"The Shoe Box" was originally published in the anthology *Christmas by the Hearth*, under ISBN 978-0-8423-0239-5, copyright © 1996 by Tyndale House Publishers, Inc., Carol Stream, Illinois.

Scripture quotations are taken from the *Holy Bible*, New Living Translation, copyright © 1996, 2004, 2007 by Tyndale House Foundation. Used by permission of Tyndale House Publishers, Inc., Carol Stream, Illinois 60188. All rights reserved.

Library of Congress Cataloging-in-Publication Data

Rivers, Francine, date
  The shoe box / Francine Rivers.
    p.   cm.
  "The shoe box" was originally published in the anthology "Christmas by the Hearth," copyright © 1996 by Tyndale House Publishers.
  ISBN 0-8423-1901-8
  I. Christmas by the hearth.   II Title.
  PS3568.I83165S46   1999
  813'.54—dc21   99-34161

Revision first published in 2010 under ISBN 978-1-4143-3888-0.

Printed in the United States of America

16   15   14   13   12   11   10
 7   6   5   4   3   2   1

Contents

How This Story Came to Be

When I first became a Christian, one of the hardest things for me to do was give my burdens to the Lord. I would worry over all kinds of things. I remember a friend talking about putting prayers in a lunch bag, and that got me thinking. One of the many jobs I had held was that of a secretary, and I remembered the in- and out-boxes. From that memory came the idea of a "God box." I took an ordinary cardboard container with a lid and covered it with beautiful wrapping paper. Then I cut a slot in the top. Whenever something was bothering me greatly and I couldn't let it go, I would write out a prayer about it. Then I would tuck the written prayer into the God box. Sometimes my husband and my children would write prayers and tuck them into the box as well. It was amazing to me how this physical exercise helped me give up worries and burdens to the Lord. Every few months I would open the box and read the prayers. What I found was a source of great joy and comfort, for many of the prayers were answered, often in completely unexpected ways.

My God box gave me the idea for "The Shoe Box." While I put worries and burdens in my box, I wanted Timmy to put blessings and praises in his box as well. It reminded me that there are all kinds of prayers—worship and praise as well as cries for help. Scripture says the prayers of believers are the sweet scent of incense to the Lord.

$\mathcal{T}$immy O'Neil came to live with Mary and David Holmes on a cloudy day in the middle of September, two weeks after school started. He was a quiet little six-year-old boy with sorrowful eyes. Not very long afterward, they wondered about the box he carried with him all the time. It was an ordinary shoe box with a red lid and the words *Running Shoes* printed on one side.

Timmy carried it everywhere he

went. When he put it down, it was always where he could see it.

"Should we ask him about it?" Mary said to her husband.

"No. He'll talk to us about it when he's ready," David said, but he was as curious as she was.

Even Mrs. Iverson, the social worker, was curious about the shoe box. She told Mary and David that Timmy had the box when the policeman brought him to the Youth Authority offices. Timmy's dad was put in prison. His mom had a job, but she didn't make enough to take proper care of Timmy. A lady in the apartment house where he lived found out he was by himself all day and reported it to the police.

"They brought him to me with one small suitcase of clothes and that shoe box," Mrs. Iverson said. "I asked him what was inside it, and he said, 'Things.' But what things he wouldn't tell me."

Even the children at Timmy's new

school were curious about the box. He didn't put it in his cubbyhole like things the other children brought. He would put it on top of his desk while he did his work.

His first-grade teacher, Mrs. King, was curious, too. "What do you have there, Timmy?"

"My box," he said.

"What's in your box?"

"Things," he said and went on with his arithmetic.

Mrs. King didn't ask him about the box again. She liked Timmy, and she didn't want to pry. She told Mary and David that Timmy was a good student. He wasn't the brightest by far, but he always did his best work. Mrs. King admired that about Timmy. She wrote a note to him about it on one of his math papers. *Other students will learn by your example,* the note said, and she drew a big smiling face on his paper and gave him a pretty, sparkly star sticker.

*M*ary Holmes learned that Timmy liked chocolate chip cookies, so she kept the cookie jar full. Timmy would come home from school on the yellow bus and sit at the kitchen table, the box under his chair. Mary always sat with him and asked him about his day while he had milk and cookies.

Timmy asked Mary one day why she and David didn't have any children of their own. Mary said she had asked God the same question over and over. She said while she waited for an answer, she was thankful to have him.

Every evening when he came home from work, David played catch with Timmy in the backyard. Timmy always brought the box outside with him and set it on the lawn chair where he could see it.

Timmy even took the shoe box with him to Sunday school. He sat between Mary and David, the box in his lap.

When he went to bed at night, the shoe box sat on the nightstand beside his bed.

Timmy got letters from his mother twice a week. Once she sent him ten dollars and a short note from his father. Timmy cried when Mary read it to him because his father said how much he missed Timmy and how sorry he was that he had made such a big mistake. Mary held Timmy on her lap in the rocking chair for a long time.

Chocolate Chip Cookies

One of my fondest memories is of my mother making chocolate chip cookies. All through my childhood, she would keep the cookie jar full of them. When I grew up and had children of my own, Mom would bake chocolate chip cookies just before I would bring our children up to Oregon for a summer visit. The first thing I would do after greeting my mother and father was head for that cookie jar! Yum! And my children were right on my heels.

After my mother and father both passed away, I started baking chocolate chip cookies for our home Bible study class. Every Tuesday afternoon, I'm in the kitchen, baking. And every time I do, I think of my mother. There is nothing like the smell of freshly baked chocolate chip cookies to stir sweet memories.

1 CUP (2 STICKS)
    BUTTER, SOFTENED
¾ CUP GRANULATED SUGAR
¾ CUP PACKED BROWN SUGAR
2 EGGS
2 TSP. VANILLA EXTRACT
1 TSP. BAKING SODA
1 TSP. SALT
2¼ CUPS ALL-PURPOSE FLOUR
1 CUP SEMISWEET CHOCOLATE
    CHIPS
¼ CUP HEATH BAR TOFFEE BITS

COMBINE BUTTER, SUGARS, EGGS, AND VANILLA EXTRACT IN LARGE BOWL. STIR UNTIL CREAMY. MIX BAKING SODA AND SALT WITH FLOUR AND ADD TO THE LARGE BOWL. STIR EVERYTHING TOGETHER, AND ADD THE CHOCOLATE AND TOFFEE BITS. (YOU CAN ADD NUTS AS WELL. CHOPPED PECANS, MACADAMIA NUTS, OR WALNUTS ARE BEST. I'VE ALSO ADDED RAISINS.)

DROP BY SPOONFULS ONTO BAKING SHEET. BAKE AT 350 DEGREES UNTIL GOLDEN BROWN.

When David came home, they took Timmy out for a pizza dinner and then to the theater to see an animated movie about a lion. Mary and David both noticed Timmy's expression of wonder and delight.

When Timmy got off the school bus the next day, he was surprised to find David waiting for him. "Hi, champ," David said. "I thought I'd come home early and share your special day." He ruffled Timmy's hair and walked with him to the house.

When they came in the kitchen door, Mary leaned down and kissed Timmy on the cheek. "Happy birthday, Timmy."

His eyes widened in surprise as he saw a big box wrapped with pretty paper and tied up with bright-colored ribbons on the kitchen table.

"It's for you, Timmy," David said. "You can open it."

Timmy put his old shoe box carefully

on the table and then opened the bigger
box with the pretty paper. In it he found
a lion just like the one in the movie.
Hugging it, he laughed.

Mary turned away quickly and fussed
with the candles on the birthday cake so
Timmy wouldn't see the tears in her eyes.

David noticed and smiled at her. It was
the first time she and David had seen
Timmy smile or laugh about anything.
And it made them very happy.

When Mary put the birthday cake on

the table and lit the candles, David took her hand and then Timmy's and said a prayer of blessing and thanksgiving. "Go ahead, Timmy. Make a wish and blow out the candles." Timmy didn't have to think very long about what he wished, and when he blew, not a candle was left burning.

SHANNON'S FUDGE

My grandmother used to make fudge every Christmas. It's nice to have my daughter, Shannon, continue the tradition!

- 3 cups sugar
- ¾ cup butter
- ⅔ cup evaporated milk
- 12 oz. semisweet chocolate chips
- 7 oz. Jet-Puffed marshmallow crème
- 1½ tsp. vanilla

This recipe is fun to put in a shaped pan, such as a tree or stocking. Line the pan with foil, lightly spray with oil, and wipe down. Mix sugar, butter, and evaporated milk in a saucepan. Bring to a rolling boil on medium heat, stirring constantly (I can't stress this enough: stir. Otherwise, it'll scorch, and you'll have to start over). Stirring constantly, boil until thermometer reaches 234 degrees, or until all the sugar has dissolved. Remove from heat. Add vanilla, chocolate, and marshmallow crème. Mix until the chocolate is melted and the color is consistent. Pour into lined and greased pan to cool. Cool to room temperature before cutting. Store at room temperature.

You can also add other flavorings, such as raspberry or peppermint. Substitute for the vanilla.

Timmy's mother came to visit every other week. She and Timmy sat together in the living room. She asked him questions about school and the Holmeses and if he was happy with them. He said he was, but he still missed her. She held him and stroked his hair back from his face and kissed him. She told him she missed him, too, but it was more important that he have a safe place to grow up. "These are nice people, Timmy. You won't grow up like I did."

Each time before she left, she always told him to be good and remember what she'd taught him. She picked him up and held him tightly for a long time before she kissed him and put him down again. Timmy was always sad and quiet when she left.

$\mathscr{F}$all came, and the leaves on the maple tree in the backyard turned brilliant gold. Sometimes Timmy would go outside and sit with his back against the trunk of the tree, his shoe box in his lap, and just watch the leaves flutter in the cool breeze.

Mary's mother and father came for Thanksgiving. Mary had gotten up very early in the morning and started preparing pies while David stuffed the turkey.

Timmy liked Mary's mother and father. Mary's mother played Monopoly with him, and her father told him funny and exciting fishing stories.

Friends came to join them for Thanksgiving dinner, and the house was full of happy people. Timmy had never seen so much food on one table before. He tried everything. When dinner was over, David gave him the wishbone. He told Timmy to let it dry and then they'd pull on it to see who would get his wish.

Decorating the Tree

Rick and I love the scent of a real tree, and I love decorating. Every year, when I open the boxes of ornaments, out pour wonderful memories. I hang pretzel-framed photos of grandchildren beside delicate glass and hand-painted German "bride" ornaments. Rick and I add to our collection when we travel, one ornament to represent each trip—a ceramic sea turtle from Hawaii, a miniature violin from Austria, a buffalo from Wyoming, a shamrock from Ireland. Swedish flags drape pine branches decorated with brass ornaments from Williamsburg and Washington, D.C. We top the tree with a crown of thorns to remind us Jesus came into the world to die for our sins. The baby born in a stable and placed in a manger is the King of kings who reigns forever.

Lil Ogden's Pie Crust

There is a lady in our church who is famous for her fantastic pies. Every year, we have a pie auction in which the youth raise money for a missions project. Lil Ogden's pies have gone for as much as seventy-five dollars. She has a servant's heart and is dedicated to prayer. And she's also a great cook!

Utensils
Large bowl
Rolling pin
Pastry blender
Measuring spoons
Flour sifter
Measuring cup
Spatula or kitchen knife
Pastry brush
Breadboard

Ingredients
1 tsp. salt
3 cups flour
1½ cups vegetable
    shortening
1 egg
1 tbsp. vinegar
5 tbsp. cold water

Mix salt and flour. Cut in shortening until fine. Mix egg, vinegar, and water together and beat with fork. Add liquid to flour mixture and stir well. Place half the dough on a floured breadboard; dust with flour and work enough into the dough to keep it from sticking. Roll out to fit size of pie plate.

FRANCINE'S APPLE PIE FILLING

THE BEST APPLES FOR A PIE ARE
GRAVENSTEIN. THEY'RE AVAILABLE
IN LATE SUMMER. WE BUY THEM BY
THE LUG AT THE ORCHARD HERE IN
SONOMA COUNTY.

6–8 APPLES (PEELED AND SLICED)
1 TBSP. BUTTER
1 TSP. CINNAMON
DASH OF NUTMEG
¾ CUP SUGAR
1 TBSP. FLOUR

$\mathcal{D}$ecember came and brought with it colder weather. Mary and David bought Timmy a heavy snow parka and gloves. His mother gave him a new backpack, and he put his shoe box in it. He carried it to school each day, and in the afternoon he'd hang the backpack on the closet door, where he could see it while he was doing his homework or when he went to bed at night.

It seemed everybody in the small town where Mary and David Holmes and

Timmy lived knew about the shoe box. But nobody but Timmy knew what was inside it.

A few boys tried to take it from him one day, but Mrs. King saw them and made them pick up trash on the school grounds during lunch hour.

Sometimes children on the bus would ask him what he had in the box, but he'd say, "Just things."

"What kind of things?"

He would shrug, but he would never say.

Simplifying Christmas

Several years ago, when storefront Christmas decorations appeared in October, our family decided to scale back, not add to the national credit card debt, and keep our focus where it belongs: on Jesus. Each family brings one gift for the entire family to enjoy throughout the afternoon: a movie, a game, or treats. After our sit-down Christmas dinner, we gather in the living room. One of our grandchildren reads the Christmas story from Luke before gifts are distributed and opened. Each grandchild receives one gift from each family. This has made for a simple, stress-free, debt-free, joy-filled celebration of Jesus' birth.

Turkey Dressing

This turkey dressing recipe was passed down from Grandma Johnson to my father-in-law, Bill Rivers. Dad Bill knew just how to cook a turkey—I never tasted one that wasn't perfect. It's been a family tradition, ever since he learned from Grandma, for each generation of men to teach the next. Dad Bill taught Rick, and Rick has taught Trevor, our eldest son. Rick also flew back East to teach our daughter, Shannon, and her husband, Rich, how to roast a Thanksgiving turkey à la Rivers. Since Dad Bill passed away, Rick has handed the baton to me. He encourages, oversees, and carves. Now that our children are grown, married, and have children of their own, new cooking traditions are developing.

2 LARGE (OR 3 SMALL) ONIONS
7 STALKS OF CELERY
1 LARGE GREEN BELL PEPPER
2 (OR 3) 6-OZ. PACKAGES
  OF CROUTONS
TURKEY GIBLETS
ENOUGH TURKEY BROTH
  TO DAMPEN STUFFING

GRIND EVERYTHING AND MIX TOGETHER. WASH INSIDE AND OUTSIDE OF TURKEY CAREFULLY. OIL INSIDE AND OUTSIDE OF TURKEY; SALT INSIDE AND OUTSIDE OF TURKEY (LIBERALLY). STUFF THE BIRD WITH YUMMY DRESSING.

The church where Mary and David Holmes took Timmy had a Christmas program each year. The choir practiced for two months to present the community with a cantata. Everyone dressed in costumes. This year part of the program was to include acting out the Nativity while the choir sang.

"We need lots of children to volunteer for the parts," Chuck, the program director, said. "The choir will sing about the angels who came to speak to the shepherds in the fields. And there's a song about the wise men who came from faraway lands to see Jesus. And, of course, we need a girl to play Mary and a boy to play Joseph."

"What about Jesus?" Timmy said.

"Latasha has a baby brother," one of the girls said. "Why don't you let her be Mary, and her baby brother can be Jesus?"

"That's a great idea," Chuck said.

Most of the children were eager to be part of the play. Even Timmy, but he was too shy to raise his hand. Chuck noticed the look on his face when all the parts were filled. He asked his helper to get the children started in a game and took Timmy aside. "We could use another shepherd in the play," he said carefully. "Would you like to be a shepherd?"

"I'd like to be a wise man."

There were already three wise men, but Chuck thought about it and nodded.

"You know, the Bible doesn't say how many wise men came to see Jesus. There might have been four. There might have been more than that. I'll talk to the lady making costumes and ask her if she can make one more for you."

The lady was very pleased to make a costume for Timmy. She spent extra time on it because she wanted it to be very special. She made a long blue tunic that went to his ankles. She made a wide multicolored sash and an outer garment like an open robe of a beautiful brocade

with purple and gold. Then she made a

turban and put a big rhinestone brooch

on the front and some colored plumes

in the top.

Christmas Lights

Jesus is the Light of the World! New traditions have developed since our children became adults, married, and blessed us with grandchildren. One new tradition is going on a "city tour" to see Christmas lights. With the local newspaper's list of the best displays in hand, we pile in our daughter's van, put on a CD or tune in to Christmas music, drive through Starbucks for coffee and cocoa, and head off on a treasure hunt to find and enjoy the light shows. It's a fun way to celebrate Jesus' birth.

Grandma Johnson's Swedish Meatballs

- 6 zwieback
- 2 eggs
- 8 oz. sour cream
- 2 or 3 onions, chopped
  butter
- 3 lbs. ground round
- 3 lbs. ground lean pork
  (boneless pork chops)
- 1 tbsp. sugar
- 1 tbsp. salt
- 1 tbsp. allspice
- 1/2 tsp. pepper
- 3/4 cup mashed potatoes

Soak zwieback in eggs and sour cream until softened; crush and mix well. Brown onions in a small amount of butter. Mix meats and spices together in large bowl. Add onions, zwieback mixture, and mashed potatoes. Mix well.

Roll mixture into balls the size of a walnut. Brown in a large skillet. Sprinkle more allspice on meat as it's cooking. Cover with water and cook over low heat for 15 minutes. Do not boil.

*W*hen the night came for the program, everyone was so excited that no one noticed that Timmy was still holding his old shoe box instead of the fancy wooden jewelry box he was supposed to carry onto the stage. Everyone did notice when he followed the other three wise men out of the wings and into the lights.

One by one the wise men approached the manger and left their gifts, but everyone sitting in the audience in the big church social hall was looking at Timmy. Timmy's mother had come to see him in the cantata. Mrs. Iverson, the social worker, had come as well. So had Mrs. King and two other teachers from Timmy's school.

They were all holding their breath when it came Timmy's turn to put his kingly offering before the manger, where the baby Jesus was sleeping. He looked like a small regal king in his royal garb, the turban and jewel on his head. The lights were on him, and the sparkles in the pretty clothes made him shine. He carried in both hands the old, worn shoe box with the red lid and the words *Running Shoes* and presented it with solemn respect to the child in the manger.

Then Timmy straightened and turned and smiled broadly at his mother, Mary and David, Mrs. Iverson, and Mrs. King and her two friends before he took his place among the other wise men at the far side of the stage.

They all let out their breath in relief, but they also sat wondering and watching Timmy. He was singing with the choir, not the least bit concerned about the precious shoe box he had left on the far side of the stage. In fact, he didn't look at it once. And they'd never seen him look so happy.

The hymn Timmy and his friends sang
in the cantata

What Child is this, who, laid to rest, on
Mary's lap is sleeping?
Whom angels greet with anthems sweet, while
shepherds watch are keeping?
This, this is Christ the King, whom shepherds
guard and angels sing;
Haste, haste to bring Him laud, the babe,
the son of Mary.

Why lies He in such mean estate where ox
and ass are feeding?
Good Christian, fear, for sinners here the
silent Word is pleading.
This, this is Christ the King, whom shepherds
guard and angels sing;
Haste, haste to bring Him laud, the babe,
the son of Mary.

So bring Him incense, gold, and myrrh,
        come, peasant, king, to own Him;
The King of kings salvation brings, let loving
        hearts enthrone Him.
This, this is Christ the King, whom shepherds
        guard and angels sing;
Haste, haste to bring Him laud, the babe,
        the son of Mary.

—William C. Dix

$\mathcal{W}$hen the cantata was over, his mother took his hand and went with him for Christmas punch and cookies. Mary and David went with them. So did Mrs. Iverson and Mrs. King and the two teachers who had come with her. They all said how proud they were of him and what a good job he did.

When it came time to go, Timmy's mother asked him if he wanted to go and get his shoe box.

"Oh no," Timmy said. "I gave it to Jesus."

They all were curious about what was inside the shoe box, but when they passed by the stage, they saw it was gone. Timmy noticed, too, but he didn't seem the least bit upset about it. In fact, he smiled.

My favorite Christmas music is Handel's Messiah. The music was composed in 1741 in twenty-four days, from August 22 to September 14. That such a beautiful work of music was written in so short a time is nothing short of miraculous! Messiah was first performed for charitable purposes in Dublin, Ireland, on April 13, 1742. Handel himself conducted. Ever since the work was heard, it has been a favorite.

I have several versions of the original and the Young Messiah, which I also love. I carry two versions in my car and listen to them while on the road. I also have a CD case full of Christmas music that I start playing as soon as Thanksgiving weekend ends. But Handel's Messiah still tops my list because of the amazing music and the even more amazing story behind it.

$\mathcal{H}$ere it is, my Lord," the angel said, kneeling before the throne of God. He held the old, worn shoe box with the words *Running Shoes* printed on it and set it at God's feet.

Jesus took it and set it upon his lap. He put his hand over it and looked out at the gathering of thousands of angels and seraphim and saints. Even they were curious about what was inside. Only he and Timmy knew.

Peter the apostle was there and, bold as always, was the only one who dared ask, "What's in that box, Lord? What has the child given you?"

"Just things," Jesus said, smiling. He had watched Timmy from the time he was conceived. He had counted every hair upon his head and knew all that was in his heart. And he had waited for the day when the child would come to him with what he had to offer.

Jesus took the top off the shoe box,

and all the angels and seraphim and
saints leaned forward as he took out one
item at a time and laid it tenderly upon
his lap.

And what they saw were *just things*—
very simple, very ordinary things:

The worn and faded silk edge of his
     baby blanket
A wedding picture of his mother
     and father
His mother's letters with a rubber
     band around them

Ten dollars

His father's note of love and apology

A math paper with a smiley face and

   a note from his teacher

A pretty star sticker

A movie ticket stub

Used birthday candles with dried

icing on them wrapped in pretty

wrapping paper and tied with a

bright curled ribbon

The big side of a broken turkey
   wishbone
A pretty red maple leaf
An old baseball
And six chocolate chip cookies

There were unseen things, too. Hopes,
dreams, prayers, and many worries and
fears. All of them were in the box Timmy
gave to the Lord.

Jesus put everything back in the shoe
box with tender care. He put the red

lid back on the box and then rested
his hands upon it as he looked at the
multitude before him. "Timmy has given
the most precious gift of all: the faith of
a child."

More angels were sent to guard
Timmy from that day forth. They never
left his side.

They were with Timmy when Mary
and David invited his mother to come
and live with them. She had a room right
across the hall from Timmy. The angels

were with him when Mary and David had a baby of their own. They were with him when his father got out of prison in time for his high school graduation. They surrounded Timmy as he grew up, married, and had children of his own.

In fact, angels surrounded him and protected him all the days of his life up until the very moment he was ushered into heaven, straight into the waiting arms of the Lord who loved him.

The Christmas Story

SELECTED FROM MATTHEW 1–2 AND LUKE 1–2

NEW LIVING TRANSLATION

This is how Jesus the Messiah was born. God sent the angel Gabriel to Nazareth, a village in Galilee, to a virgin named Mary. She was engaged to be married to a man named Joseph, a descendant of King David. Gabriel appeared to her and said, "Greetings, favored woman! The Lord is with you!"

Confused and disturbed, Mary tried to

think what the angel could mean. "Don't be afraid, Mary," the angel told her, "for you have found favor with God! You will conceive and give birth to a son, and you will name him Jesus. He will be very great and will be called the Son of the Most High. The Lord God will give him the throne of his ancestor David. And he will reign over Israel forever; his Kingdom will never end!"

Mary asked the angel, "But how can this happen? I am a virgin."

The angel replied, "The Holy Spirit will come upon you, and the power of the Most High will overshadow you. So the baby born to you will be holy, and he will be called the Son of God. What's more, your relative Elizabeth has become pregnant in her old age! People used to say she was barren, but she has already conceived a son and is now in her sixth month. For nothing is impossible with God."

Mary responded, "I am the Lord's servant. May everything you have said

about me come true." And then the
angel left her.

While she was still a virgin, she became
pregnant through the power of the Holy
Spirit. Joseph, her fiancé, was a good man
and did not want to disgrace her publicly, so
he decided to break the engagement quietly.

As he considered this, an angel of the
Lord appeared to him in a dream. "Joseph,
son of David," the angel said, "do not be
afraid to take Mary as your wife. For the
child within her was conceived by the Holy

Spirit. And she will have a son, and you are to name him Jesus, for he will save his people from their sins."

All of this occurred to fulfill the Lord's message through his prophet:

"Look! The virgin will conceive a child!
    She will give birth to a son,
    and they will call him Immanuel,
        which means 'God is with us.'"

When Joseph woke up, he did as the angel of the Lord commanded.

A few days later Mary hurried to the hill country of Judea, to the town where Zechariah lived. She entered the house and greeted Elizabeth. At the sound of Mary's greeting, Elizabeth's child leaped within her, and Elizabeth was filled with the Holy Spirit.

Elizabeth gave a glad cry and exclaimed to Mary, "God has blessed you above all women, and your child is blessed. Why am I so honored, that the mother of my Lord should visit me? When I heard your *greeting, the baby in my womb jumped for*

joy! You are blessed because you believed

that the Lord would do what he said."

Mary responded,

"Oh, how my soul praises the Lord.

   How my spirit rejoices in God

      my Savior!

For he took notice of his lowly

   servant girl,

   and from now on all generations will

      call me blessed.

For the Mighty One is holy,

and he has done great things for me."

Mary stayed with Elizabeth about
three months and then went back to
her own home.

At that time the Roman emperor,
Augustus, decreed that a census should be
taken throughout the Roman Empire. (This
was the first census taken when Quirinius
was governor of Syria.) All returned to
their own ancestral towns to register for this

*census. And because Joseph was a descendant
of King David, he had to go to Bethlehem
in Judea, David's ancient home. He
traveled there from the village of Nazareth
in Galilee. He took with him Mary, his
fiancée, who was now obviously pregnant.*

*And while they were there, the time
came for her baby to be born. She gave
birth to her first child, a son. She wrapped
him snugly in strips of cloth and laid him
in a manger, because there was no lodging
available for them.*

That night there were shepherds staying in the fields nearby, guarding their flocks of sheep. Suddenly, an angel of the Lord appeared among them, and the radiance of the Lord's glory surrounded them. They were terrified, but the angel reassured them. "Don't be afraid!" he said. "I bring you good news that will bring great joy to all people. The Savior—yes, the Messiah, the Lord—has been born today in Bethlehem, the city of David! And you will recognize him by this sign: You will find a baby wrapped snugly in strips of cloth, lying in a manger."

Suddenly, the angel was joined by a vast host of others—the armies of heaven— praising God and saying,

"Glory to God in highest heaven,
and peace on earth to those with
whom God is pleased."

When the angels had returned to heaven, the shepherds said to each other, "Let's go to Bethlehem! Let's see this thing that has happened, which the Lord has told us about."

They hurried to the village and found Mary and Joseph. And there was the baby, lying in the manger. After seeing him, the shepherds told everyone what had happened and what the angel had said to them about this child. All who heard the shepherds' story were astonished, but Mary kept all these things in her heart and thought about them often. The shepherds went back to their flocks, glorifying and praising God for all they had heard and seen. It was just as the angel had told them.

About that time some wise men from eastern lands arrived in Jerusalem, asking, "Where is the newborn king of the Jews? We saw his star as it rose, and we have come to worship him."

King Herod was deeply disturbed when he heard this, as was everyone in Jerusalem. He called a meeting of the leading priests and teachers of religious law and asked, "Where is the Messiah supposed to be born?"

"In Bethlehem in Judea," they said, "for this is what the prophet wrote:

'And you, O Bethlehem in the land
        of Judah,
    are not least among the ruling cities
        of Judah,
    for a ruler will come from you
        who will be the shepherd for my
        people Israel.'"

Then Herod called for a private meeting with the wise men, and he learned from them the time when the star first appeared. Then he told them, "Go to Bethlehem and search carefully for the child. And when you find him, come back and tell me so that I can go and worship him, too!"

After this interview the wise men went their way. And the star they had seen in the east guided them to Bethlehem. It went ahead of them and stopped over the place where the child was. When they saw the star, they were filled with joy! They entered the house and saw the child with his mother, Mary, and they bowed down and worshiped him. Then they opened their treasure chests and gave him gifts of gold, frankincense, and myrrh.

When it was time to leave, they returned to their own country by another route, for God had warned them in a dream not to return to Herod.

About the Author

New York Times best-selling author
Francine Rivers began her literary career
at the University of Nevada, Reno,
where she graduated with a bachelor of
arts degree in English and journalism.
From 1976 to 1985, she had a success-
ful writing career in the general market,
and her books were highly acclaimed by
readers and reviewers. Although raised in
a religious home, Francine did not truly
encounter Christ until later in life, when
she was already a wife, a mother of three,
and an established romance novelist.

Shortly after becoming a born-again

Christian in 1986, Francine wrote *Redeeming Love* as her statement of faith. First published by Bantam Books, and then rereleased by Multnomah Publishers in the mid-1990s, this retelling of the biblical story of Gomer and Hosea, set during the time of the California Gold Rush, is now considered by many to be a classic work of Christian fiction. *Redeeming Love* continues to be one of CBA's top-selling titles, and it has held a spot on the Christian best-seller list for nearly a decade.

Since *Redeeming Love*, Francine has published numerous novels with

Christian themes—all best sellers—and she has continued to win both industry acclaim and reader loyalty around the globe. Her Christian novels have been awarded or nominated for numerous honors, including the RITA Award, the Christy Award, the ECPA Gold Medallion, and the Holt Medallion in Honor of Outstanding Literary Talent. In 1997, after winning her third RITA Award for inspirational fiction, Francine was inducted into the Romance Writers of America Hall of Fame. Francine's novels have been translated into more than twenty different languages, and she enjoys best-seller status in many foreign countries, including Germany, the Netherlands, and South Africa.

Francine and her husband, Rick, live in northern California and enjoy time spent with their three grown children and taking every opportunity to spoil their grandchildren. Francine uses her writing to draw closer to the Lord, and she desires that through her work she might worship and praise Jesus for all He has done and is doing in her life.

Visit her Web site at www.francinerivers.com.

BOOKS BY BELOVED AUTHOR
FRANCINE RIVERS

The Mark of the Lion series
(available individually or as a boxed set)
A Voice in the Wind
An Echo in the Darkness
As Sure as the Dawn

A Lineage of Grace series
(available individually or in an anthology)
Unveiled
Unashamed
Unshaken
Unspoken
Unafraid

Sons of Encouragement series
The Priest
The Warrior
The Prince
The Prophet
The Scribe

Marta's Legacy series
Her Mother's Hope
Her Daughter's Dream

Children's Titles
The Shoe Box
Bible Stories for Growing Kids
(coauthored with Shannon Rivers Coibion)

Stand-alone Titles
Redeeming Love
The Atonement Child
The Scarlet Thread
The Last Sin Eater
Leota's Garden
And the Shofar Blew
The Shoe Box (a Christmas novella)

www.francinerivers.com

have you visited
tyndalefiction.com
lately?

Only there can you find:

⟶ books hot off the press

⟶ first chapter excerpts

⟶ inside scoops on your favorite authors

⟶ author interviews

⟶ contests

⟶ fun facts

⟶ and much more!

Sign up for your **free** newsletter!

Visit us today at: tyndalefiction.com

Tyndale fiction does more than entertain.

⟶ *It touches the heart.*

⟶ *It stirs the soul.*

⟶ *It changes lives.*

That's why Tyndale is so committed to being first in fiction!

TYNDALE FICTION

CP0021